The
Christmas
Strangers

Marjorie Thayer
Pictures by Don Freeman

Library of Congress Cataloging in Publication Data

Thayer, Marjorie.
    The Christmas strangers.

    "A Golden Gate junior book."
    SUMMARY: During a snowstorm on Christmas eve,
three strangers arrive at the Clinton family's log
cabin in the Michigan territory.
    [1. Christmas stories. 2. Frontier and pioneer life—
Fiction] I. Freeman, Don. II. Title.
PZ7.T3299Ch   [Fic]   75-38575
ISBN 0-516-08719-3

12 R 87 86 85

For Marion

Ben stared out of the window at the falling snow. It was falling faster now. The snow had begun in the night when everyone was asleep in the little cabin at the edge of the clearing. Everyone, that is, except Pa. Before sunup the day before, Pa had hitched Rusty to the wagon and set out for town. Pa was to get the supplies for tomorrow's Christmas dinner. And the Christmas presents! This year there would be real presents, store-bought presents for them all.

It had been a good year for the Clinton family. There was enough money from Pa's trapping and other things to have a real Christmas, almost like the ones Back East. Ben could just remember how Christmas was before the family moved to Michigan territory and built the log cabin.

"Do you think Pa can make it back in time for Christmas?" Eight-year-old Joe, Ben's younger brother by two years, stood beside him. The two boys peered anxiously at the white flakes that were beginning to make a curtain between the cabin and the dark trees that ringed it.

"I hope so, Joe," Ben answered, sounding worried. "It's almost Christmas Eve. If Pa doesn't come soon there won't be enough daylight to hunt a turkey for dinner tomorrow."

"And what about the presents he's bringing?" Joe asked. "The girls sure will be disappointed if they don't get those china dolls on Christmas morning. And I want that ball! I've waited months for it!"

"Not as long as I've waited for my bowie knife.

Pa said this year I'd be big enough to have it. He
knows I want it more than anything."

Ben moved from the window. His twin sisters, Maggie and Beckie, who had just turned six, were playing with their rag dolls near the warm cooking stove. Their mother sat in her rocking chair mending one of the children's stockings.

"Ma," Ben asked for the tenth time that day, "do you think Pa will come soon? We won't have any Christmas if he doesn't get here before long."

Ma folded her work, then joined her two sons. Outside the snow fell steadily. The gray sky seemed to darken as they watched.

Their mother did not speak for a moment. Then she said quietly, "Boys, I only hope your father hasn't tried to come home this day. The wagon track between here and town will be completely snow-covered by now. The wagon couldn't possibly get through the drifts. I pray he never started back at all but is safe and warm by the stove in Bob Jenkins' store."

"But Ma!" Both boys spoke at once. "What'll we do for Christmas?" Ben wailed. "Pa promised we could go with him to hunt a wild turkey for dinner tomorrow."

"And we won't have any presents, none at all!" cried Joe, his voice squeaking in disappointment.

"No presents?" The twins, who had dropped their playthings to listen, echoed Joe's words, then began to cry. "Isn't Santa Claus coming?" they wanted to know between sobs.

"Now look here, children, all of you." Ma spoke sharply. "Quiet down, girls. You're too big to be such cry-babies. I can't believe that one of you is selfish enough to wish your father to run into danger. If this snow keeps up and the wind starts to blow, we may have a real blizzard before long. Just pray your father is safe and will return to us when the storm is over. We'll make the best of things and have Christmas anyway."

"But how, Ma, how?" Ben looked unbelieving. "We haven't even got anything special to eat. Pa promised he'd bring us candy—"

"We'll have some kind of Christmas tree at least,"

his mother interrupted. "Boys, do you see that big pine tree right at the edge of the clearing?" Ma pointed a finger. "It has long low branches and one of them will make a fine Christmas tree. Ben, you and Joe take Pa's hatchet and go out and cut it for us. You can shovel a path through the snow that far. Put on your coats and mittens and wear your mufflers. Be quick about it! It'll be dark real early with this storm."

She turned to the twins who had stopped crying and were looking at her, wide-eyed. "Maggie and Beckie," she said cheerfully, "you're going to help decorate the tree. How would you like to pop some corn? We can string it on some of my knitting yarn and make pretty white garlands."

When the boys opened the door snow swirled into the room. Ma seized her broom and began to sweep it up. Then she and the twins watched from the window as Ben and Joe shovelled away at the snow, clearing enough of a path to reach the pine tree. Ma

had to keep wiping away the steam on the inside of the windowpane so that they could look out.

Popping corn was great fun. Ma took some hard yellow kernels from a jar she kept on the shelf above the stove and put them in an iron pan. She set the pan on the hottest part of the stove, letting the twins take turns jiggling it back and forth. Soon there was a small pop, then another and another, as the kernels burst into fluffy white flowers. Ma poured them into a bowl and added more kernels to the hot pan. In a few minutes there was a heaping dish of popcorn.

"Please, Ma, can we eat some now while it's hot?" Maggie and Beckie were dancing up and down with delight.

"You can each have a small handful," Ma answered, "and so can the boys when they come in. The rest we'll save for the Christmas tree."

A great pounding on the door signalled that the boys were back. Ma opened the door and there they stood, covered with snow. Even their eyelashes were frosted. Each carried one end of a long, snow-covered

pine branch. "Merry Christmas!" shouted Ben. "We did it, Ma! But hurry up and let us in before we freeze to death out here."

"Shake the snow off that branch and yourselves

first," Ma laughed. "There's enough snow on you to drown us when it melts."

Soon the pine branch was standing upright in a corner of the cabin. The single branch wasn't full enough for a real tree, of course, but its dark green needles were plentiful, bright and shiny. Their spicy odor soon began to scent the warm room.

Ma showed the little girls how to string the popcorn on long strands of knitting yarn. Ben and Joe took turns looping them among the green needles.

"Now what we need are some bright-colored ornaments," Ma said. "I know just what we'll make them from. I've been saving scraps for a new quilt, but I'm going to take the very prettiest pieces and turn them into Christmas tree decorations instead. Joe, run and fetch my scrap bag. Now where did I put my scissors?"

It wasn't long before Ma's swift fingers had made nearly a dozen decorations. There were stars, blue and white and red and yellow ones. Ma cut out a little round snow man from a piece of white cloth and from a bright green piece fashioned a tiny ornament in the shape of a Christmas tree. Then she helped the twins to cut out stars of their own.

Outside the wind picked up and began to blow. It howled around the cabin and from time to time seemed to hurl itself against its sides. Indoors shadows gathered in the corners. Ma laid down her scissors and rose to light the lamp. "We'll finish decorating the tree after supper," she said. "Ben, you and I had best hurry out to feed and milk old Betsy before it gets any darker or windier. She's safe enough in the shed but she'll have to be milked and given enough hay until morning. Joe, you go down in the root cellar and get us some potatoes and onions for dinner tomorrow. There'll be enough smoked deer meat for all of us."

"Some Christmas dinner!" grumbled Joe. "It won't make up for the turkey we counted on."

"Ma," Ben said excitedly, "I'll bet I could shoot a turkey! I know how to use Pa's gun." He looked up at the rifle on its pegs above the door. Pa always

kept it there, cleaned and loaded, ready for use in an emergency.

"Nonsense," Ma said. "You'd have to go goodness knows how far into the woods to even see a turkey. You'd be lost and half-frozen in no time. Pa will get us one when he comes home. I'm only thankful we have enough wood for the stove so that we can cook and keep warm. You'll have to bring more from the shed in the morning, but we have plenty for this night. We'll have an early supper and after we've finished the tree we'll sing some Christmas carols. Then I'll read you the Christmas story, just as Pa would do if he were here."

When supper, beans with a bit of salt pork, was over Ma quickly washed the dishes. The girls dried them and put them away. Ma lighted some extra candles because it was Christmas Eve and, though the wind howled outside, the little cabin was warm and cheerful.

Everybody helped to fasten the bright cloth ornaments to the makeshift Christmas tree. The twins were especially happy with the result. They kept telling everybody how beautiful their Christmas tree was. "Santa Claus will come, won't he, Ma?" Maggie asked.

"Yes, but he's going to be late this year on account

of the storm," Ma answered. "But you can each hang one of your clean stockings on the tree for him to find when he does come."

The twins scrambled to find the stockings. They reached as high as they could to hang them up.

"Ma," Ben said when at last their mother was settled in the rocking chair by the stove, "before we start singing the carols tell us how it was at Christmas Back East when Grandma and Grandpa came. I was awful little then but I can still remember some of it."

"Yes, tell us," the twins cried as they huddled close to the rocking chair.

"Well, you've heard it all before many times," Ma said. "Of course we lived in a town then and we had a lot more things than we have out here. We could buy sugar and flour at the store most any time we wanted to. Before Christmas I'd bake for days, pies and cakes and Christmas cookies. The day before Christmas we'd take big baskets full of good things to families in town who were too poor to have much of a Christmas dinner.

"Grandma and Grandpa always came by Christmas Eve. Grandpa would hitch his matched pair of horses to the sleigh. My, how the sleigh bells on their harnesses would ring out! After supper we'd decorate the Christmas tree. Then the carolers—people in the town who had good singing voices—would come to our door to sing carols. Then it would be time to walk through the snow to the church for Midnight Service."

Ma broke off abruptly. "But look here, children," she said, a little catch in her voice. "It's Christmas Eve here and now in Michigan, not in Vermont, and we have a lot to be grateful for. We may not have much, but we're together—and Pa will come as soon as the snow stops and it's safe to travel. We're warm and well sheltered and we have enough to eat. Pity the poor Indians out in the storm with only their wigwams to protect them. They don't even know it's Christmas!"

"Why don't they, Ma?" Maggie asked, looking surprised.

"Because they have other customs and worship gods of their own," Ma answered.

"Don't they even know about the Baby Jesus being born on Christmas? Everybody knows that story," Beckie declared.

"Nobody's ever taught them, poor creatures. But let's not talk about Indians," Ma said. "Let's see if we remember *Away In A Manger*. That's a good Christmas song to begin with. Ben, you're the oldest. You start us off."

Ben did, though not quite on pitch, and soon they were all singing. They sang *Hark! The Herald Angels Sing* and *The First Noel* and *O Tannenbaum*, until Ma reminded them that it was past bedtime. "The twins have sat up later tonight than ever they have," she said. "I'll read you the Christmas story from the Bible and then we'll all get a good night's rest. Perhaps tomorrow—oh, let us hope so—the snow will have stopped and Pa will be home!"

Joe and the twins watched as Ma took the Bible down from its place on the highest shelf. Ben wan-

dered over to the window. Though he knew it was foolish, he couldn't quite give up the notion that, by some miracle, Pa might get through the storm tonight. He rubbed away the steam and pressed his face against the windowpane. Ma opened the Bible and began to read.

"And it came to pass in those days that there went out a decree from Caesar Augustus that all the world should be taxed. And all went to be taxed, everyone unto his own city. And Joseph also went up from Galilee, out of the city of Nazareth, unto Judea, unto the city of David, which is called Bethlehem, to be taxed with Mary, his espoused wife, being great with child. And so it was that, while they were there, the days were accomplished that she should be delivered. And she brought forth her firstborn son and wrapped him in swaddling clothes and laid him in a manger because there was no room for them in the inn. And there were in the same country shepherds—"

"Ma!" Ben interrupted, his voice hardly more than a whisper. "There's a face right up against the window! I think it's an Indian."

Ma closed the Bible before she spoke. "Nonsense," she said. "In this storm? There isn't an Indian within twenty-five miles of us. There's no one there, children. Ben's imagining things."

But then it came—a loud thud against the door, then another and another. Ben sprang for the rifle above the door. "No, Ben, no!" Ma cried. "Not on

Christmas Eve! Someone out there is lost in the storm. We'll have to see who it is.''

Slowly, cautiously, inch by inch, Ma opened the door, just enough to peek out. ''They *are* Indians,'' she whispered. ''Two of them. Oh, *why* isn't Pa here?''

She stood for a moment, her hand on the door latch. ''Ben,'' she said, ''take the rifle down. Hold it ready but don't aim it. Girls, run up the ladder to the loft and stay there. Joe, stand here by me. *I'm going to let them in.''*

All their lives Ben and Joe would remember what happened then. The two figures that stumbled, almost fell, into the room were so covered with snow that little else could be seen but snow and their red-brown faces. One was a young man, the other a young woman. In the woman's arms was a small bundle which she hugged against her breast. Without looking at anyone she hurried straight to the stove. She laid the bundle on the floor, then knelt beside it. Quickly, but gently and carefully, she unwrapped it. Inside

the bundle was a tiny red-brown baby.

The man spoke then. "Lost," he said in a harsh, low voice. "Lost in storm. Baby sick."

The baby opened black eyes and began to cough, a tiny hoarse sound in the quiet room. The woman picked it up and held it closer to the stove. It seemed to have trouble breathing.

"The poor little thing, it's got the croup," Ma cried. "Out in all this terrible storm it's a wonder it's alive! Ben, put up that gun and set a kettle of water on the stove to boil. Joe, bring blankets from our beds in the loft. I know just what to do for it," she told the mother. "I've had four children of my own."

Fear showed, naked and plain, in the woman's face. She bent over the baby, shielding it with her body. "Don't be afraid," Ma said. "Don't you understand? I won't hurt your baby. It's got the croup and I'm going to cure it."

Now it was nearly midnight, almost Christmas morning. It was quiet inside the cabin. The baby

30

slept, wrapped in warm blankets, beside the stove. It was breathing easily now. The hot steam kettle and the camphor Ma always kept on hand, to inhale and to rub chests with, had done their work. The young Indian and his wife were stretched out on the floor, asleep, covered with the heavy furs Ma had given them.

Upstairs in the loft Ma, Joe and the twins slept at last. Only Ben was wide awake. He could not stop

thinking about all that had happened—or how scared he'd been, even with Pa's gun in his hands. But the Indians had been scared too. He could still see the woman's terrified face as Ma reached toward her baby. But Ma had gone ahead and saved it anyway.

Ben remembered how surprised he'd been that the young man spoke their language, at least enough to tell them that his people were on the way west to a new village. When the storm came, he and his wife and baby had gotten separated from the rest. They had been afraid they'd freeze to death until they saw the light from the cabin in the clearing.

When she was sure the baby would be all right and was asleep, Ma fed the father and mother. She gave them the smoked deer meat she'd been saving for tomorrow. Joe told about not having a wild turkey to cook for Christmas dinner. "Christmas, a great feast day," Ma had tried to explain. The Indian had smiled and nodded as though he too knew about Christmas.

A small sunbeam made its way through a chink in the attic and touched Ben on the nose. He opened one eye, then sat up. For a minute he couldn't think what was different. The wind had stopped! He looked at the streak of light across his quilt covering. The sun was shining. It was Christmas—and Pa would be home! Suddenly he remembered last night and the Christmas Eve visitors.

The rest of the family were still asleep. He decided not to wake them. Shoes in hand, he crept down the ladder. The Indian woman was fast asleep beside the stove. Her baby slept close beside her. The man was not there.

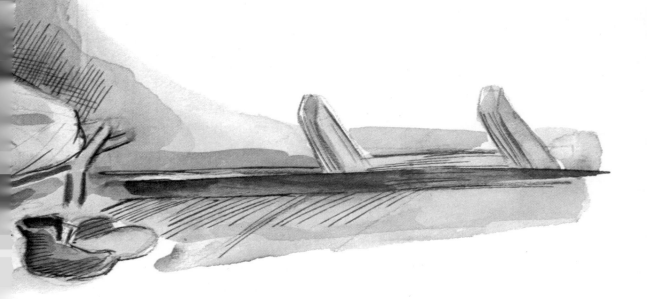

Ben didn't know what made him look up to the pegs above the door where Pa's rifle was kept. The space was empty. He knew that last night he had put the gun back, carefully, while Ma was helping the baby. He thought about the bowie knife and wished that he had it now. He must wake Ma at once.

There was a noise above his head. Joe came down the ladder, followed by the twins who nearly tumbled over one another in their haste to get down. "Where's the baby? Where's the baby?" they shouted. "We want to see the baby!"

The Indian woman woke up and Ben saw again the fear in her face. But then she smiled and held the baby toward the little girls. First Maggie, then Beckie, took one of his tiny hands and felt his fingers curl around theirs.

Ma was downstairs now and Ben knew he wouldn't have to tell her for she had seen at once what was missing. But she said cheerfully, "Merry Christmas, all of you. Thank heaven the storm's

over. You boys hustle out and see to Betsy, then bring in the wood. I'll stir up the fire and make a pot of corn meal mush for breakfast."

While Ben was putting an armload of wood beside the stove Ma whispered to him, "I've tried to ask the woman where her man is but she doesn't understand and I don't think she knows anyway. Ben, don't let on to the others, but I'm frightened."

Ma served the corn meal mush in big wooden bowls. The Indian woman joined them. In their wonder over the baby the little girls had forgotten all about not having any Christmas presents.

They were just finishing breakfast when they heard the knock on the door. Ben was quicker than Ma in getting to the window to look out. "Oh Ma," he cried, "it's the Indian. He's carrying Pa's gun and a great big turkey!"

When he came inside everybody could see how pleased the Indian was at what he had done. He smiled and smiled at them all. "Good dinner now," he said, pointing to the turkey.

"Yes, and you must stay long enough to have it with us before you travel on," Ma told him. "We'll have a real Christmas dinner now!"

Later in the day, just as everybody was enjoying a second helping of turkey, the sound they had been waiting for came at last.

"Merry Christmas! Merry Christmas!" Pa called as he opened the door. He was grinning from ear to ear as he put down the big sack he carried over one shoulder.

Everybody hugged Pa all at once. Then Joe and the twins rushed to open the sack. Ben waited to listen while Ma told Pa in a whisper how the Indians came to be there. When she had finished telling him everything Pa smiled and held out his hand. He and the young man shook hands for what seemed a long time.

For the moment Ben had nearly forgotten about his bowie knife. But there it was, long and sharp and shining. Joe had his ball and Ma a fine plaid shawl.

Maggie and Beckie had never seen anything as splendid as their dolls. They were exactly alike and they had beautiful china heads, with black eyes and wavy black china hair. Their cheeks were bright pink and they had smiling red mouths.

There were new clothes for everyone too. There was red and white striped candy, lots and lots of it. And there was something else, a surprise nobody had even dreamed of, at the bottom of Pa's sack—a shining red and black checker board with gleaming round black and red checkers. "A game for the long evenings in winter," Pa told them. "I'll teach you all how to play, even the twins."

There had never been such a Christmas!

They all made so much noise that they woke up the baby. He cried and his mother hurried to pick him up. Ben wasn't sure whether it was Maggie or Beckie who said, "But we forgot the baby! He hasn't any Christmas presents."

Of course the baby was too young to know and his mother and father didn't quite understand either, but

they smiled and nodded when, a little later, the
children brought him his gifts. Joe had found a warm
knitted muffler to wrap him in and there was a little
knitted cap Ma had once made for one of the twin's
dolls. Beckie brought him three tiny pine cones she
had been saving and Maggie took the yellow star she
had cut out from the Christmas tree and laid it in
his hand.

Ben didn't know what to give the baby. He didn't
seem to own anything a baby would want. Then he

thought about the baby's father, how he'd gone out in the snow and hunted the turkey for them. He picked up his new knife and balanced it in his hand. He looked at it hard. Then he held it out to the Indian. "This is for you," he said. "Merry Christmas."